CB137309

THE CHILDREN'S CLASSICS Collection

Dados Internacionais de Catalogação na Publicação (CIP) de acordo com ISBD

C319a Carroll, Lewis.
Alice's adventures in Wonderland / Lewis Carroll. - Jandira, SP : W. Books, 2025.
120 p. : 12,80cm x 19,80cm. - (Classics).

ISBN: 978-65-5294-127-5

1. Literatura inglesa. 2. Fantasia. 3. Clássicos. 4. Imaginação. 5. Aventura.
I. Título. II. Série.

2025-2473 CDD 820
CDU 821.111-3

Elaborada por Lucio Feitosa - CRB-8/8803
Índice para catálogo sistemático:
1. Literatura inglesa 820
2. Literatura inglesa 821.111-3

The Children's Easy Classics 10 Book Collection: Series 1
Text © Sweet Cherry Publishing Limited, 2024
Inside illustrations © Sweet Cherry Publishing Limited, 2024
Cover illustrations © Sweet Cherry Publishing Limited, 2024

Based on the original story by Lewis Carroll,
adapted by Gemma Barder
Illustrations by Grace Westwood

© 2025 edition:
Ciranda Cultural Editora e Distribuidora Ltda.

1st edition in 2025
www.cirandacultural.com.br
No part of this publication may be reproduced, stored in a retrieval system, or transmitted in any form or by any means, electronic, mechanical, photocopying, recording, or otherwise, without written permission of the publisher.
This book is a work of fiction. Names, characters, places, and incidents are either the product of the author's imagination or are used fictitiously, and any resemblance to actual persons, living or dead, business establishments, events, or locales is entirely coincidental.

Alice's Adventures in Wonderland

Lewis Carroll

W. Books

Alice

A young girl

The White Rabbit

A rabbit that is late

The Hatter

A hatmaker with a broken pocket watch

The March Hare

A hare that hosts a tea party

The Duchess

The Queen's sister

The Queen of Hearts

An angry queen

The King of Hearts

An angry king

The Knave of Hearts

A playing card accused of theft

Chapter One

Alice sat in the shade of a large oak tree at the bottom of her garden. It was a warm, dreamy afternoon, and she had been in the same spot for hours. Her sister was reading aloud, but the book was so dull that Alice was struggling to stay awake. She yawned, thinking how much nicer it would be to be back in her room, with her cat, Dinah, curled up in her lap …

Just as Alice was about to drift off, she spotted a white rabbit running past the oak tree. Seeing a rabbit was not unusual, as they often liked hopping through the garden – but *this* rabbit was running on two legs rather than four. Not only that, it was wearing a smart red waistcoat and a tiny pair of spectacles on the end of its nose.

It was not every day that Alice saw a rabbit like *that*, so, with a glance towards her sister to check that she wasn't looking, Alice ran after it. She followed the rabbit through the garden gate and across the fields, where it stopped suddenly. Alice caught up just in time to see the rabbit take a shiny silver pocket watch from its waistcoat pocket. 'Oh dear! Oh dear!' it said. 'I shall be too late!'

Alice was so shocked to hear the rabbit talk that she nearly fell over. By the time she regained her balance, it had disappeared.

Where could he have gone? thought Alice.

Searching the grass, she came across a large rabbit hole. 'Mr Rabbit?' Alice called into it. There was no reply, and the rabbit did not reappear.

Alice got down on the ground and peered into the darkness. The hole looked very deep.

'Excuse me!' she called again. 'Is there a smartly dressed rabbit down there?'

Before she could wait for a reply, the soft ground beneath Alice gave way and she fell into the inky emptiness below. Down, down, down.

Alice screamed. She could not tell which way was up and which was down. It was so dark, she could not even see her own hand in front of her face. But as Alice continued to fall, she noticed her surroundings getting brighter. She could see that the hole was lined with shelves, and on the shelves were candles, jars and lots and lots of books. It gave her something to look at as she fell – which she did for a very long time. Far too long to stay scared. After her fear had melted away, in fact, she even started to get a little bored.

I wonder how long I have been falling for? she thought. *Perhaps I will fall all the way to the centre of the earth? Or further.*

Just as Alice was thinking how she would introduce herself to people in Australia (if she happened to fall so far that she landed on the other side of the earth), Alice finally stopped falling.

Chapter Two

Alice landed with a small bump on a pile of twigs and leaves. She stood up and brushed the dirt off her light-blue dress and black patent shoes. She looked up at the hole above her. It extended so far that the many shelves disappeared into darkness the higher they went.

Where have I ended up? she thought, looking around at where she had landed.

Alice found herself in a long, narrow hallway with a black and white marble floor and doors lining each side. She looked all around for the White Rabbit, but there was no sign of him anywhere. *Perhaps I should try one of these doors?* Alice thought. *It might lead to a staircase or some way out, I suppose?* But each door Alice tried was locked shut.

Just as Alice was about to attempt climbing back up the rabbit hole, she spotted a glass table at one end of the room.

On top of the table sat a tiny brass key and a blue glass bottle.

'A key!' Alice cried. 'It must be for one of the doors!'

Alice eagerly tested each door with the key, but every one remained locked.

The key was much too small.

Alice sighed with frustration. It was then that she saw a door she had not noticed before. It was no bigger than a mousehole, but it was the only door left. The key *must* fit it.

Alice knelt on the ground and peered through the tiny keyhole. She saw a beautiful garden and her heart filled with joy. Gardens meant people, which must mean that there was a way for her to

get home beyond the door. But how? She was much too big to fit through it.

Perhaps the little blue bottle will help? Alice thought.

She returned to the table and picked up the bottle. The small luggage label attached to the neck read:

Alice was a sensible girl most of the time. But so many strange things had happened to her already that she was open to one more if it would help her get home.

The liquid inside the bottle tasted delicious. It was like cherry pie, custard, pineapple, roast turkey and hot buttered toast all mixed together. Alice was so distracted by it that she did not realise she was shrinking!

Chapter Three

Alice got smaller and smaller and smaller. Soon she was so small that she could easily fit through the little door that led to the beautiful garden. She rushed back across the marble floor – which took a lot longer now that she was so tiny – and seized the doorknob. She rummaged in the pocket of her dress for the key. Her heart sank.

She had left the key on the table.

The table that now towered far, far, *far* above her.

Tears welled in Alice's eyes. 'Come now!' she told herself sternly. 'No good will come from crying about it!'

As she wiped away the tears, Alice spotted a little box at the foot of the table. Inside, there was a small cake with raisins arranged on top that read:

‘Curiouser and curiouser,’ said Alice, taking the cake in her hand. ‘Well, perhaps if the drink made me small, the cake will make me big again!’

Alice took a little bite from the corner of the cake. Nothing happened, but the cake was as delicious as the drink, so Alice decided to finish it. If nothing else, it would make her feel a lot better.

When Alice had stopped chewing, she wiped the crumbs from her mouth – and got quite a shock. The roof of the narrow room was pressing on the top of her head!

'Goodness me!' cried Alice in alarm. 'Now I am far *too* big!'

She fumbled to pick up the little key to place

it in her gigantic pockets, although she still had no idea how she was going to get through the door.

At that moment, Alice heard footsteps. One of the doors opened – and out came the White Rabbit! He was now wearing a very smart jacket over his waistcoat, and he was holding a fan and a pair of white gloves.

'Oh dear, oh dear,' said the rabbit. 'The Queen is going to be so cross if I am late!'

'Excuse me, Mr Rabbit!' called Alice from her great height.

The rabbit jumped in fear

when he saw the giant girl. He dropped his fan and gloves and disappeared through the door to the garden, using his own set of special keys to lock it on the other side. Alice was a little annoyed at the rabbit for running off, and also a little sorry for making him drop his gloves and fan. Wherever he was going must be very important and she did not want him to be improperly dressed. But she could hardly go after him and help now, could she?

'It's all so hopeless!' Alice said, as tears once again filled her eyes.

This time, she could do nothing to stop them. Great big teardrops splashed onto the marble floor and made a puddle by her feet. Alice closed her eyes and used the rabbit's fan to cool her face, but still the tears came. Her shoes and socks were getting wet. Suddenly, Alice opened her eyes and found she was now up to her waist in water!

Chapter Four

'The fan!' Alice realised. 'The fan has made me shrink down again!'

She stopped fanning herself immediately. She did not want to turn into a speck of dust, after all. The only trouble was, Alice was now so small that her puddle of tears was like a huge lake in comparison. She was going to have to swim.

Alice could see the top of the little door to the garden peeking above the salty waves. If she could only open the door, all the water would drain out and she would be swept away with it.

She swam as well as she could, but Alice soon got distracted by a brown creature bobbing on the waves next to her. At first, she thought it might be a walrus or a seal, then she remembered how tiny she was and realised it was a mouse.

The mouse looked at Alice in such an angry way that it made her stop swimming for a moment to apologise for her part in the situation.

'Hello,' she began. 'I'm terribly sorry about all this. These are my tears, you see.' The mouse continued to glare at Alice. 'What am I doing?' laughed Alice. 'First, I talk to rabbits, now mice. Just wait until I tell Dinah!'

'Who's Dinah?' asked the mouse.

Alice was a little startled that the mouse had replied, but she

had already heard a rabbit talk that day and she did not want to appear rude.

'Erm, Dinah is my cat,' she replied.

'A cat!' squeaked the mouse, suddenly splashing about in fear. 'Where? *Where?*' The mouse started swimming as fast as her four little legs would carry her. Alice swam after her.

'No, no! There's no cat here! I was talking about my cat at home!' she called. 'She is a terribly nice cat. She wouldn't harm you!'

Still swimming, Alice and the

mouse finally bumped into the little door to the garden. Alice reached into her pocket for the key.

'Here, I can help,' she said, hoping to get back on the mouse's good side. Alice turned the key in the door. As she pushed it open, Alice and the mouse were carried through into the garden on a wave of tears.

The garden was just as beautiful as Alice had seen through the keyhole. Tall flowers loomed over her head in all different colours and sweet smells filled the air.

As Alice turned to look at the mouse, she saw that the creature had scampered off. She was all alone again.

Alice was just deciding which path she should take through the garden, or if she should start shouting for help, when the White Rabbit reappeared.

'Where are they? Where are they? The Queen will be so cross with me!' he muttered.

'It's you!' Alice cried, delighted to see someone familiar in the garden. The White Rabbit looked at Alice for a moment.

'Mary Ann? What are you doing here?' he asked. Alice looked behind her to make sure the rabbit was not talking to anyone else. 'Go home this instant and fetch me a new pair of gloves and a fan.'

Alice soon realised that the rabbit was calling *her* Mary Ann.

Chapter Five

'I'm not Mary Ann,' said Alice, as politely as she could. 'I am trying to find my way–'

'We do not have time for this, Mary Ann!' said the rabbit, interrupting Alice. 'The Queen will be very cross with me if I am late. Go! Go!' The rabbit began shooing Alice down one of the garden paths with his little white paws and Alice had no choice but do as she was told.

A short way down the path, she came to a perfect little rabbit-sized cottage. *This must be the place*, Alice thought.

Because she was still small in size, she slipped through the front door easily and began to look around. She was in the entrance hall where a green door had been left open. Alice gently pushed it and it led into the kitchen. There was a small stove with an even smaller kettle on top. She spotted a familiar-looking blue bottle on the rabbit's kitchen table. It was similar to the one that had been on the table in the hallway with the black-and-white floor, but without any label. Alice remembered just how delicious the first drink had been.

One small sip won't make me that *much smaller*, she thought to herself.

Alice took the tiniest sip from the blue bottle, but this time she did not shrink. In fact, she *grew*!

And she did not stop growing until one leg stuck out of the front door of the cottage and one leg stuck out of the back door. Her arms, meanwhile, stuck out of the windows. Both her arms and legs were out of her control, they knocked over everything in their path as Alice grew.

'Oh dear,' sighed Alice. 'Everything is back to front and upside down in this place!'

To make matters worse, Alice could now see a very cross-looking white rabbit hopping up the lane towards his cottage.

'Mary Ann! What have you done!' gasped the rabbit.

Before Alice could even begin to explain, the rabbit started burrowing in the flower beds in the garden that surrounded his cottage. He emerged with his paws full of pebbles.

'I am awfully sorry, Mr Rabbit!' called Alice in a panic. 'But I really don't think I deserve to have pebbles thrown at me!'

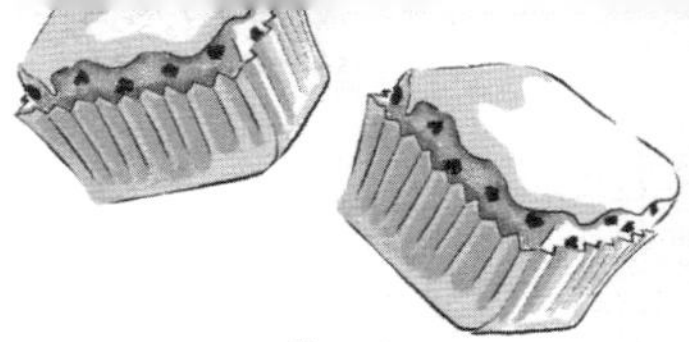

The rabbit rolled his eyes and tossed one into Alice's hand. To her amazement, the pebbles were not really pebbles at all. They were small cakes! With a bit of effort – after all, her arms were stuck through the windows and her head was up in the attic – Alice nibbled on the cake. Immediately, she started to shrink back to normal size – or at least normal for this strange new world down the rabbit hole.

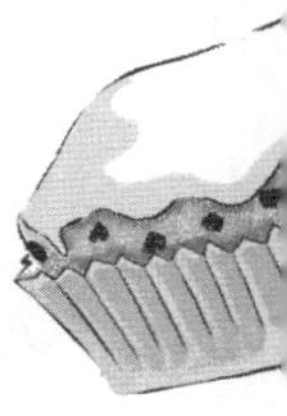

Alice rushed out of the cottage door to thank the rabbit, but he was gone. Alice sighed. She wished she could fix the rabbit's cottage for him, but she did not know how or even where to start. All that she could do was carry on down the path and keep wondering how she was ever going to find her way out of this strange place.

Chapter Six

Alice had been following the path for ages and she had found herself walking through a wood. Alice noticed clouds of blue smoke rising from somewhere just up ahead. Further on, the smoke turned purple, then red, then orange.

How curious, thought Alice.

Soon, she found herself stood at the bottom of a giant mushroom. On top sat a blue caterpillar smoking a long pipe.

'Excuse me!' Alice called. 'I wonder if you could help me?'

The Caterpillar turned slowly to look down at Alice. He took a puff of his pipe and blew a yellow stream of smoke into the air.

'Whooo. Aaare. Yooou ...' the Caterpillar said, slowly.

Alice thought for a moment. 'I knew who I was when I woke up this morning,' she said. 'But I have changed so many times since then that I don't quite know who I am now.'

The Caterpillar took another long puff on his pipe. This time the smoke came out in green circles.

'Hooow ridiculous,' he said. '*I* know who *I* am.'

Alice frowned. She tried to think the best of people whenever she could, especially when meeting someone for the very first time, but this caterpillar was being rude.

'Well,' she said a little crossly, 'you might think differently when you turn into a butterfly. Then *you* won't know who *you* are either!'

'I *always* know who I am,' replied the Caterpillar. 'The question is, who would *you* like to be?'

Alice sighed. 'Well, I suppose I would like to be the same person I was when I began,' she said. 'I would like to be taller. Being small is no fun at all.'

'Excuse me!' said the Caterpillar. 'Being small is perfectly *wonderful*.'

Alice looked down at her shoes, ashamed at herself for insulting the Caterpillar when he was the only one around to help her.

'I shall give you two pieces of advice,' the Caterpillar said. 'First: one side of this mushroom will help you grow and the other will help you shrink. Second: keep your temper!' With that, the Caterpillar slunk away, leaving a trail of blue smoke behind him.

Alice stared at the mushroom. One side would make her grow.

The other would make her shrink. She reached up and broke a piece of mushroom off from each side.

But which side does what? Alice wondered.

Carefully, she took a bite from the mushroom in her right hand. In an instant, Alice was smaller than she had ever been. Blades of grass towered over her.

'Goodness!' she said.

Alice took a big bite out of the mushroom in her left hand. Now she was taller than the clouds! A family of pigeons flew past her nose and flapped their wings in fright.

'This is getting silly,' Alice said.

Gradually, she took tiny nibbles of each mushroom piece until she felt she was herself again. She hadn't been her human size in a long time. Then she placed the last of the mushroom pieces in her pockets, just in case.

After all, who knew what would happen next?

Chapter Seven

Walking through the woods felt endless to Alice. She had not seen the Caterpillar again or the White Rabbit. She missed Dinah and wondered if her sister had looked up from her book long enough yet to notice that Alice had gone.

It was at that moment that Alice spotted another small cottage. The top of the chimney stack looked as though it would come up no further than Alice's shoulder. There was a light in the window and Alice hoped that whoever was inside might be able to help her.

'But not if I knock on the door as my normal size,' said Alice. 'Whoever lives inside must be quite small indeed.'

Alice reached into her right-hand pocket and took a small bite of the mushroom until she was just the right size for the door.

Before Alice did anything, she was mesmerised by a peculiar sight that waddled around the corner.

A fish!

It was a fish walking on its tail fins as though they were legs, dressed in the sort of uniform Alice had only seen in pictures of footmen at Buckingham Palace. The fish knocked on the door of the cottage and a short woman in fine clothes answered.

'Good day, Duchess. I have an invitation from the Queen!'

footman

A household servant, traditionally for a royal family, who attends a carriage or serves a table.

announced the fish, giving the woman a golden envelope. 'Croquet in the palace gardens this afternoon!' Alice noticed that as the fish spoke, bubbles popped out his mouth and floated into the air.

The Duchess took the invitation and closed the door, while the fish waddled away. Alice rubbed her

croquet

An outdoor game in which mallets are used to drive wooden balls through square-topped hoops towards a goal.

eyes in disbelief. She had seen some very strange and wondrous things so far in this land, but that was by far the strangest.

When Alice had pulled herself together, she knocked on the door.

The Duchess answered again. This time she was holding a small bundle in her arms, cradling it like a baby.

'Well, are you coming in or are you not?' she said.

'We're far too busy for you to just stand there like that.'

The Duchess swept back inside, singing to the bundle in her arms. Alice followed her a little uncertainly. The kitchen she entered was hot and filled with the smell of pepper. Alice sneezed. A cook was standing over a huge pot that bubbled on a stove, and the Duchess was barking orders from her seat at the kitchen table. Warming itself by the stove was a beautiful cat that seemed to be smiling from ear to ear.

‘There, there now, pig!’ said the Duchess, bobbing the bundle up and down. Alice thought this was a very strange name for a baby. Then again, everything was strange here.

‘Why is your cat smiling?’ Alice asked.

‘Because he’s a Cheshire Cat, of course. All Cheshire cats grin like that,' replied the Duchess. 'But I don't have time to discuss this with you. Cook! The soup needs more pepper! Here, you take pig,' the Duchess said, passing the bundle to Alice. Startled, Alice took it in her arms. 'I'm off to get ready for croquet with my sister!'

Alice could not stand the pepper-filled air any longer. She wrapped the bundle in its blanket and took it back outside.

'Poor little thing,' she said, finally looking down at the baby. 'Goodness! You're not a baby!'

Alice gasped. 'At least, not a *human* baby.'

Alice knelt down and unwrapped the startled-looking piglet. It nodded gratefully at Alice before disappearing into the woods.

Chapter Eight

Alice decided not to go back into the Duchess's house. The smell of the peppery soup had made her nose tickle, her eyes sting and she was sure she would not find any help in there anyway.

'Can I help?' said a voice. It was the Cheshire Cat. Alice had not seen it leave the

Duchess's house, but it was now perching on a tree branch ahead. Alice could not understand how it had made it there so quickly.

'I am wondering which way I should go,' said Alice.

'In that direction,' said the cat, waving his paw, 'is the Hatter. And in that direction,' he waved his paw again, 'is the March Hare. It doesn't matter which one you choose. They are both mad.'

‘How do you know?’ asked Alice. It seemed rather rude to call someone “mad” just like that.

‘Because we are all mad here!’ said the cat. ‘Even you, or you would not be here.’ With that, the cat vanished.

On any normal day, Alice would be astonished to see a cat vanish into thin air, but today she had seen so many impossible things that she took it in her stride. She looked at the two paths the cat had pointed out to her and decided to walk towards the March Hare. She had been to a hatter before to get a fancy bonnet made for church, but she had never met a march hare.

'One more thing,' said the Cheshire Cat, reappearing in front of Alice so suddenly that she jumped.

'I wish you would not do that!' said Alice, a little annoyed. 'What is it?'

'Are you going to play croquet with the Queen? If so, you will see me there.'

'I would like to very much,' said Alice. Croquet was one of the games she loved to play with Dinah. 'But I haven't been invited.'

The Cheshire Cat slowly began to disappear again until all that was left was his shining toothy grin.

'Well, I have often seen a cat without a grin before,' said Alice. 'But I have never seen a grin without a cat!'

After even the Cheshire Cat's grin had vanished, Alice continued walking until she came upon yet another little house. She could hear singing and laughter, and as she got closer it sounded as if someone was having a tea party …

Chapter Nine

Alice came upon a large dining table laid out beautifully for tea in the garden of the March Hare's house. At one end of the table sat the hare and, Alice

guessed, the Hatter. She guessed this because of the tall green top hat he was wearing. Between them lay a dormouse fast asleep on a currant bun.

Alice's stomach rumbled. She had not eaten a bite since breakfast apart from a little cake and a nibble of a mushroom.

The March Hare and the Hatter seemed to be having a deep discussion about something. Trying not to disturb them, Alice quietly took a seat at the opposite end of the table.

'No room!' shouted the March Hare.

'No room!' shouted the Hatter.

Alice looked about her at the empty seats that lined each side of the table. 'Excuse me,' she said. 'But I think you'll find there is plenty of room.'

'And who asked you to sit down?' said the March Hare, hopping to Alice's side. Alice had no reply. No one had asked her to sit down, but she was hungry and tired.

'It's OK, missy,' called the Hatter. 'You can have some tea if you answer a simple riddle.'

Alice clapped her hands. 'Oh good! I love riddles!' she said, listening closely.

'Why is a raven like a writing desk?' asked the Hatter.

Alice paused. Usually, she could work out riddles quite quickly, but this one was tricky. She was still wracking her brain for an answer when the Hatter pulled out his pocket watch.

‘Now!’ he said. ‘Back to the matter in hand – my watch. We’ve tried spreading butter on it and dipping it in tea, but nothing works. It still says six o’clock.’

'Six o'clock?' cried the dormouse, suddenly waking from her sleep. 'Everybody switch!'

Suddenly, the March Hare, hatter and dormouse all got up from their seats and moved three spaces down the table. When they had settled, they all looked at Alice expectantly.

'Well, what are you waiting for?' they chimed.

'Oh, I see!' said Alice. And she got up and moved along the table three spaces too. 'Your watch is broken so it is always tea time and you keep moving around, which is why there is no room at the table!'

'Very clever!' said the Hatter. 'But do you know why a raven is like a writing desk?'

'I don't know,' Alice replied, puzzled and weary. 'Please tell me the answer?'

'I haven't the faintest idea!' said the Hatter.

Alice was getting frustrated with her new companions. She was thinking about carrying on through the woods when she spotted a door in the trunk of a tree nearby.

'Thank you for having me,' said Alice politely. 'But I think I shall be on my way.'

Chapter Ten

Alice stepped through the door in the tree and found herself in a beautiful garden filled with red rosebushes. She wandered dreamily among them. The flowers were so beautiful they looked as though they were made of velvet. She reached out to touch one of the soft petals and was surprised when her fingers came away wet.

'What are you doing?' said a

panicked voice behind the bushes. As Alice looked closer, she saw that it was a playing card. Not any old playing card, but a playing card that was as tall as she was. A playing card that could speak. A playing card that happened to be holding a paint brush with paint dripping from the bristles.

'Are you *painting* the roses?' asked Alice, who could not quite believe what she was seeing.

Just then, another playing card came rushing towards them carrying a large tin of red paint.

'Seven! The Queen will be here any minute and we haven't finished!' said the second playing card.

'I know, Four,' said Seven. 'And this little girl has been touching the roses we've already painted! Look, she's smudged one!'

Alice felt bad for messing up the playing cards' work. 'Maybe I can help you,' she said. 'But *why* exactly are you painting the roses?'

Four looked around himself to make sure no one was listening. Then, in a low voice, he said, 'It is for the Queen of Hearts. She hates anything but *red* roses. We accidentally planted a row of white roses last year and we need to paint all the blooms before the Queen arrives or …' Four stopped speaking and gulped.

'Or what?' asked Alice.

'Or it is off with our heads!' replied Seven.

Alice laughed nervously.

'Surely the Queen would not cut off your heads for a little mistake!'

'She has chopped off heads for far less,' said Four. 'We need to get this finished as soon as we can or else.'

Seeing how scared the poor playing cards were, and being someone who always tried to be as helpful as she could, Alice found a spare paint brush and started to paint the roses red. As they finished the final rosebush, a trumpet sounded in the garden and marching feet could be heard coming towards them.

'The Queen!' cried Seven, hiding the paint tins and brushes. 'She's coming!'

Chapter Eleven

A parade of playing cards began to march past Alice, Four and Seven. First came the clubs, then the spades, then the diamonds and lastly the hearts. At the very end were the kings and queens of each suit, with the Queen of Hearts herself being carried on a golden throne. For some reason, although she was not entirely sure why, Alice stood to attention in the way she had seen soldiers do in the army when someone important walked past.

'WAIT!' bellowed the Queen. 'Put me down!'

Seven and Four looked at each other with terror in their eyes. The Queen came closer and sniffed the rosebushes with her large turned-up nose. She plucked one of the blooms and

held it in the air the same way Alice's mother did when she was checking for a smudge on a glass.

At that moment, a trickle of red paint made its way onto the Queen's hand and her face turned pink with rage. 'These roses have been *painted*!' she roared. 'PAGE! Get here at once!'

Alice was stunned to see the White Rabbit scurrying along to meet the Queen with a trumpet in his hand. He glanced at Alice, but did not say anything to her.

'Your Majesty,' said the rabbit. 'What can I do for you?'

'Four and Seven have been *painting* roses in my garden. Off with their heads!' said the Queen, waving her hand in the cards' direction.

'Oh, but you can't!' squealed Alice. The Queen of Hearts turned to look at her as though seeing her standing there for the very first time.

'How *dare* you tell the Queen what she can and can't do! Off with *your* head too!' said the Queen.

The White Rabbit hopped from foot to foot and cleared his throat. 'Your Majesty, if I may,' he began. 'The girl is just a child. Perhaps she can keep her head a little longer and she might learn how to behave?'

The Queen looked Alice up and down and thought for a moment. 'Hmm, perhaps you are right,' she said. 'She can join us for croquet instead! A good game of croquet might sort out her manners. But as for Four and Seven – it's off with their heads!'

'At once, Your Majesty,' said the rabbit. Alice was about to protest. She did not want the poor playing cards to lose their heads! But as she watched, she could see that the rabbit was shooing them away to hide behind a bush instead. The Queen was too busy climbing back onto her throne to notice.

'Have they lost their heads?' she called as she was carried away.

'Oh yes, Your Majesty!' lied the rabbit.

Alice breathed a sigh of relief.

Chapter Twelve

Alice smiled at the White Rabbit. He had saved Four and Seven from losing their heads and she was grateful.

'Mary Ann, what are you doing here?' the rabbit asked. He still seemed to think that Alice was someone else.

That or she simply looked like a Mary Ann to him. Alice decided not to correct him. He had done a very nice thing and he looked like he was very busy dealing with the Queen. She did not mind being Mary Ann for a little while longer.

'I am trying to find my way home,' Alice said.

'Well, you will need to play croquet first,' he replied. 'If the Queen has asked you, then you simply must.'

Alice and the rabbit went to a lush green lawn that had been laid out with hoops for a game of croquet.

'Is the Duchess here?' Alice asked.

‘Oh no, the Queen had her imprisoned,’ said the rabbit. ‘They argued over which flamingos they were going to use.’

Alice frowned. ‘Flamingos?’ she asked.

‘Shush now, Mary Ann,’ said the rabbit, hurrying off. ‘The game is about to begin!’

Alice watched as the kings and queens of each suit picked out a mallet and ball to play with. As Alice stepped closer to pick

Mallet

A tool similar to a hammer. Often has a wooden handle and a large barrel-shaped head. Used in croquet with a long handle to drive the ball.

out her own mallet, she noticed something rather strange about the croquet equipment. All the mallets were, in fact, flamingos. And all the balls were tiny balled-up hedgehogs.

As Alice glanced around the playing lawn, she saw that the hoops were not really hoops at all.

They were playing cards standing on all-fours with their middles bent over in an arch.

'This is the most curious game of croquet I have ever seen!' said Alice.

Then, as she watched the game, it got even curiouser. Whenever a ball (hedgehog) was struck with a mallet (flamingo) and looked as though it was about to sail through a hoop (card), the hoop would move out of the way or the ball would scurry off in the wrong direction. This continued until it was Alice's turn to take a shot.

Alice lined up her flamingo's long neck with the hedgehog. 'I will try not to hit you very hard,' she whispered to the creatures, feeling bad for them. But each time she tried to hit the hedgehog, her flamingo would suddenly bend its head to look up at her, making it impossible.

'What are you doing?' asked Alice.

The flamingo shrugged. 'Queen's orders.'

Alice had the feeling this game was not being played fairly, but she had no choice but to keep swinging.

Chapter Thirteen

When Alice finally managed to hit the ball (hedgehog), she was pleased to see it head for one of the hoops – or rather one of the poor playing cards. But just as the hedgehog was about to go whizzing through the hoop, the playing card suddenly fell flat and Alice's hedgehog rolled straight over it.

Alice could feel herself getting rather cross until she remembered what

the Caterpillar had told her. *Keep your temper.* She looked across the lawn at the terrible Queen of Hearts who ordered executions and locked her own sister, the Duchess, in a tower. It would not be wise to upset her.

'Good day to you,' said a voice, just above Alice's head.

At first, it seemed as though the voice was coming from the air itself. Then, bit by bit, the Cheshire Cat appeared as though curled up on a cloud.

executed

Historically, when someone was killed as punishment by law.

'I see you were invited after all,' he said, grinning his usual grin.

'I was. But I am not enjoying the game very much,' Alice said. 'I think the Queen might be …' Alice wanted to say that she thought the Queen might be cheating, but she had a sudden feeling that the Queen was standing right behind her. 'That is, I think the Queen might be the best croquet player I have ever seen!'

The Queen wafted past, smiling at Alice. The King of Hearts trailed after her.

‘Whatever is that?’ asked the King, pointing at the Cheshire Cat bobbing about in the air. ‘And why does it have that look on its face?’

‘He’s smiling, Your Majesty,’ said Alice, wishing that the cat would stop smiling just for a moment, or perhaps disappear altogether.

‘What on earth is it smiling about? And why is it looking at me?’ said the King, getting increasingly cross. ‘How dare you look the King of Hearts in the eye!’

‘A cat can look at a king,’ said the Cheshire Cat, who had begun to float above the King’s head.

‘My dear, I demand you order another execution for this rude cat!’ shouted the King. And because she liked nothing better, the Queen immediately bellowed: ‘OFF WITH ITS HEAD!’

Alice could not understand why the cat continued to smile. He must not have understood what was about to happen.

'Oh no, please don't hurt him,' said Alice, who loved cats more than anything.

'It is all OK, Alice,' said the cat, dreamily. 'They can have my head. Look – here it is.'

The cat's body vanished, leaving just his smiling face to float around them.

The Queen opened her mouth, but no order came out. After all, how could she cut off someone's head when there was only a head in the first place?

Chapter Fourteen

Once the Queen was satisfied that it was pointless to cut the head off a cat with no body, she grew tired and went back to her game. Alice was starting to get tired, too. She was tired of the Queen and the whole strange land she ruled over.

Alice looked around for another door. A door that might take her back to the rabbit hole. Perhaps then she could find a way to climb back up and get back to her sister under the oak tree. She might even be in time for tea.

'TRIAL!' shouted the White Rabbit, suddenly. Anyone who was still playing croquet stopped and looked at him. 'Now begins the trial of the Knave of Hearts!'

A trial? thought Alice. She had never seen a trial in real life before – although she had read about them in books. She had to admit, she was quite interested to see what a trial in this strange land would look like.

trial

The act of hearing a case in court to decide whether or not a person has broken a particular law.

‘Oh, Mr Rabbit?’ Alice said, hurrying along behind the rabbit. ‘Who is the knave and what has he done to be put on trial?’

‘Mary Ann, I don’t have time to explain,’ said the White Rabbit. ‘You can come along and watch if you like.’

Alice’s curiosity got the better of her. She decided to stop looking for a way home just for a while and followed the White Rabbit towards a large, important-looking building. Inside, it looked just like any other courtroom Alice had read about. There was a seat behind a large desk that overlooked two rows of smaller desks. Along each side of the courtroom were rows and rows of seats, a little like where the choir might sit in a church.

Alice silently took a seat and waited for the judge, who just so happened to be the Queen of Hearts herself, to take her seat.

'Bring in the prisoner!' the Queen shouted, and out of a trapdoor in the floor, the Knave of Hearts appeared. He looked very sorry for himself and his hands were chained together.

Goodness! thought Alice. *He must have done something very bad indeed!*

The White Rabbit produced a scroll of paper and began to read from it. 'Knave of Hearts! You are accused of stealing twelve of Her Majesty's finest jam tarts!'

Jam tarts! thought Alice. *What a small crime to make such a fuss over!*

'I call our first witness,' said the White Rabbit. 'I call the Hatter!'

Chapter Fifteen

Alice's eyes widened as the small man in the large green top hat, whom she had met at that rather strange tea party, appeared. He was still holding the same teacup as when she had last seen him. Alice hoped the tea was not the same too, as it would be terribly cold by now.

The Hatter took a seat on a tall stool where the Queen could stare at him with her dark, accusing eyes.

Alice noticed that the Hatter's hand trembled as he lifted his tea cup to his lips to take a sip.

'Now, Mr Hatter, what have you to say on the matter?' said the King of Hearts, pacing up and down in front of the Hatter's stool.

'I think the March Hare said something to the dormouse about the tarts and the tea,' began the Hatter. 'But then the dormouse fell asleep and the hare bounced about, and nothing really happened until Alice turned up.'

Alice felt her cheeks burn red. What did *she* have to do with any of it?

'But what about the tarts?' demanded the Queen of Hearts.

'Well, the dormouse likes tarts, but only in winter, and the March Hare is allergic to round things, so ...'

'ENOUGH of this nonsense!' cried the Queen. 'Next witness!'

The Hatter quickly left the stool and poured himself another cup of tea from a teapot in his inside jacket pocket.

Next to sit on the stool, Alice

recognised the Duchess's cook in his stained apron and floppy chef's hat.

'Can you confirm that it was you who made the tarts?' said the King, as he began to pace the courtroom once more.

'Aye,' said the cook.

'And what were they made of?' asked the King.

'Jam and pepper – just as the Queen likes 'em,' said the cook.

Alice rolled her eyes. This cook seemed to be obsessed with putting pepper in everything.

With all this talk of tarts, Alice's

tummy began to rumble again. She reached into the left-hand pocket of her dress and discovered that she still had some of the Caterpillar's mushroom.

A tiny bite won't hurt, Alice thought.

'And who do *you* think stole the tarts?' the King asked the cook.

'Well, I dunno,' the cook replied. 'Maybe that young girl who came and stole the pig from us? What was her name? Alice!'

Chapter Sixteen

At the mention of her name, Alice shrank into her seat as well as she could. This was difficult after eating the mushroom. She was now tall enough that her knees knocked against the seats in front of her.

The Queen was drumming her fingers on her desk and the noise seemed to echo around the whole courtroom.

'I have made a decision!' the

Queen said at last. 'Knave, you are free to go!'

Alice was delighted by this turn of events. Perhaps the Queen was starting to see some sense after all. You cannot simply go chaining people up just for eating some jam tarts!

'Now, seize the girl called Alice and bring her to me!' roared the Queen.

Alice was so shocked that she sprang to her feet. It was only

then that she realised the last bite of mushroom had made her so tall that her head nearly reached the roof of the courtroom.

'Make yourself shorter at once!' shouted the Queen. 'I need to look you in the eye when I sentence you!'

Alice folded her arms. 'Now wait just a minute!' she said. 'I don't know much about the law, but even I know that you must reach a verdict

sentence
A punishment for a particular crime decided in a court of law.

verdict
A decision or opinion. In court, it is the judge who decides if a person is guilty or not.

before you sentence someone – and I haven't even been given a trial.'

'SILENCE!' shouted the Queen, her face turning almost as red as the hearts on her dress. 'I am the Queen and I can do as I like! I say you stole the tarts and I say off with your head. CARDS!'

At the Queen's demand, rows and rows of playing cards of all different suits charged towards Alice. The only trouble was that Alice was now far, far bigger than the playing cards – and *any* of the characters she had met since falling down the rabbit hole. The more they charged, the more Alice simply swept them away, as though brushing dry leaves from the hem of her dress.

Distantly, she heard the White Rabbit calling to her – 'Alice! Alice!' – which was odd. The White Rabbit had never called her Alice before. He had always called her Mary Ann. But still the voice carried on. 'Alice!' it called. 'Oh, Alice, do wake up. You have been asleep for *such* a long time!'

Chapter Seventeen

Alice blinked; sunlight blinded her as it danced though the branches of a tree above her. As she shaded her eyes, she could see her sister sitting next to her, picking leaves off her dress.

'You fell asleep!' said Alice's sister. 'I bet you hardly heard any of my story, did you?'

Alice realised she was back under the shade of the old oak tree in her garden once more.

Alice stood up, feeling dazed. She looked at her feet to see if any of the Queen's playing cards were still attacking her. All she saw was grass and the twisting roots of the oak tree under her black patent shoes.

'The Queen,' she said. 'She was just here ...'

'What are you talking about, Alice?' said her sister, tucking her book under her arm and frowning.

'The Queen, the White Rabbit and the Hatter, they were all just here a moment ago,' replied Alice.

Alice's sister sighed. 'You've been dreaming again, Alice,' she said. 'Come along. Mama will want us home for tea.'

Alice followed her sister, but she was still looking about her. She was certain that the rabbit would appear at her side at any moment, or that the Cheshire Cat would start bobbing around in the air above her head.

'It all felt so real …' she said, feeling slightly sad. 'It was a little frustrating and a *lot* silly, but … well, quite wondrous. That's it! It was like a wonderland!'

Alice's sister giggled. 'A whole wonderland under an oak tree in the garden?' she said. 'I think that's the best dream you've had yet.'

Alice sighed. Perhaps it was just a dream after all. The more she thought about it, the less real it became. Rabbits in waistcoats, vanishing cats, a murderous queen playing croquet with flamingos. It all sounded unbelievable.

Just then, Alice put her hands into the pockets of her dress. She could feel something soft in each and when she pulled out her hands again – yes – there they were! Pieces of the Caterpillar's mushroom.

Had it been real after all? All she had to do was take a little bite to find out ...

Lewis Carroll

Charles Lutwidge Dodgson, who went by the pen name of Lewis Carroll, was born in Cheshire in 1832. Growing up, Carroll invented many stories and games for his friends and siblings to play. From a young age, Carroll wrote short stories and poems and contributed to his family's magazines. It is said that inspiration for *Alice in Wonderland* came from Carroll's time in Oxford. Now, it is one of the most popular children's books in the world.